Text copyright © Anthony Masters 1997
Illustrations copyright © Alan Marks 1997

First published in Great Britain in 1997
by Macdonald Young Books
an imprint of Wayland Publishers Ltd
61 Western Road
Hove
East Sussex
BN3 1JD

Find Macdonald Young Books on the internet at http://www.wayland.co.uk

The right of Anthony Masters to be identified as the author of this
Work and the right of Alan Marks to be identified as the illustrator
of this Work has been asserted by them in accordance with the
Copyright, Designs and Patents Act 1988.

Designed and Typeset by Backup Creative Service, Dorset DT10 1DB
Printed and bound in Belgium by Proost International Book Production

British Library Cataloguing in Publication Data available

ISBN 0 7500 2211 6

ANTHONY MASTERS

The Haunted Lighthouse

Illustrated by Alan Marks

MACDONALD YOUNG BOOKS

Chapter One

The seals crowded the rock below Seal Rock Lighthouse. They gazed up at Philip who stared back in amazement. He had never seen so many, their dark skins glistening, their eyes watching him closely.

A winter storm was brewing. The sky was black and the waves were getting bigger, pounding on the reef that stretched out to sea like a row of sharp teeth.

He was standing in the top chamber where the light used to revolve, warning ships off the rocks with its bright white beam. But now that the big lamp had been shut down, the lighthouse had become a museum.

Philip and his father had moved there a month ago when his father had become curator. Philip's grandfather had been the last of the lighthouse keepers, but he had drowned whilst out fishing in his boat years before Philip was born. Philip often thought about him, wondering what his life must have been like.

Philip didn't like living at the lighthouse. He was lonely without his friends and felt uneasy being so close to the sea. It was spooky.

The biggest seal was on the very top of the rock now. His eyes seemed to be boring straight into Philip's. Philip felt uncomfortable and wondered why. Then he remembered how local people believed that inside the seals were the souls of the drowned.

Philip told himself the legend was just a made-up story. But the idea wouldn't go away and his uneasiness increased.

Lightning split the sky in a series of jagged flashes, and then a growl of thunder came from far out to sea. In the eerie silence that followed, Philip heard the sound of his father's footsteps ringing out on the spiral staircase that led to the top chamber.

Gasping for breath, Philip's father reached the top chamber, but when he caught sight of the seals he looked as scared as Philip. "I've never seen so many before."

"Neither have I," said Philip. "What are they all doing there?"

"It's just like your grandad used to say..." His father hesitated.

"What did he say, Dad?" Philip asked irritably, wondering why his father hadn't finished what he was saying.

"When the seals gather on Seal Rock, there'll be a shipwreck," he replied reluctantly and then added, "It's just an old story, of course."

They both gazed down at the rock that crouched under the lighthouse. The thunder growled again and the lightning lit the sky, making the seals look white and ghostly.

Chapter Two

Philip first heard the footsteps on the stairs while he was reading in bed. He sat up and listened. What was Dad doing, going up to the chamber again?

Then to his surprise, his father opened the door and came into the bedroom. So he wasn't on the stairs after all.

But someone was. Philip could hear pounding feet on the staircase above that began to break into a run. He could also hear the gasping of breath, and anxious mutterings.

"Can't you hear those footsteps, Dad?" Philip was confused.

"What footsteps?" His father listened and then shrugged. "It's the storm. Hailstones most likely."

"They're on the staircase. Going up."
Philip was really scared now.

"I can't hear anything, it's just the
storm." With that, his father said
goodnight and went out. As he did so, the
footsteps stopped as suddenly as they had
begun. Philip was left wondering if he
had imagined what he had
heard. Maybe he was
feverish.

Philip tried to sleep but only managed to doze uneasily.

Suddenly he sat bolt upright, shivering and shaking all over. He could hear the footsteps again. This time they were even louder and more urgent than before and the rasping of breath was much closer.

Philip nervously got up and ran down the staircase, only to find his father

reading a paper in the living room.

"Can't you sleep?" his father asked crossly.

"I just wanted a glass of water," snapped Philip. If only they were back home and not living in this creepy lighthouse, he would be able to sleep.

Whilst he was in the kitchen, Philip listened carefully but could only hear the booming of the sea. Reluctantly, he went back to bed again.

Chapter Three

Philip's head was too full of footsteps and thunder and homesickness to try to sleep again. The flashes of lightning made his furniture look as if it had suddenly been painted white.

Eventually Philip drifted off into another light doze from which he soon woke abruptly, hearing the footsteps yet again. This time the gasping seemed even nearer than before.

She'll be on the rocks if she doesn't change course. The strange voice rang inside

his mind.

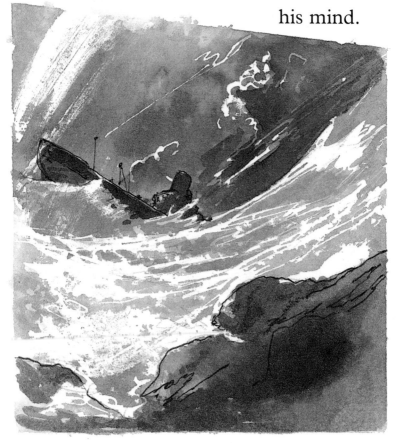

Philip was terrified. What was happening to him now? Had he made the words up? Imagined them? He sat up in bed, his heart racing. Tiptoeing fearfully to his bedroom door he opened it slowly. Someone was running up the spiral staircase, their footsteps hammering the iron rungs.

The figure was misty, shadowy, hardly there at all. Then the shape became more solid and Philip could see a tall man wearing a cap and a thick sweater. He had a white beard and a straggling moustache, and Philip could even see the sweat streaming down his face.

The figure began to fade away, and Philip shook with fear. What was going on? He knew he had to find out.

Philip ran towards the staircase and then more slowly and cautiously began to climb to the light chamber at the top. It was a long way up and the higher he got, the colder he became.

Halfway up he stopped, too scared to continue. He clung to the rail as hard as he could, shivering violently, as if he were under the ice of a frozen lake. Gradually the feeling passed, and he began to climb again.

Chapter Four

Somehow, Philip forced himself on, and the faster he climbed the warmer he began to feel. But when he reached the top the cold feeling came back much more strongly and Philip found it hard to catch his breath. He was freezing again now and his icy fingers fumbled with the latch. At last he managed to open the door.

The light chamber was filled with a floating fog and he could hardly see anything. Gradually it cleared, and Philip could make out the shimmering figure of the man in the sweater gazing out into the storm. He was wearing a cap that looked exactly like the keeper's cap in the museum display.

Still standing by the door, not daring to move, Philip could just see out through the huge glass windows. The seals were lying on the rock in the boiling surf, but the big seal he had noticed earlier was no longer there.

The rain was lashing down and the wind was wailing and shrieking. Philip peered into the distance, trying to see what the keeper was staring at.

Then, dimly glowing through the driving rain he could just make out a ship's lights, and he remembered the voice that had so frighteningly entered his mind.

She'll be on the rocks if she doesn't change course.

Right now the ship was heading straight for the reef.

Slowly turning away from the windows, the keeper began to drift towards the great lamp that had once revolved, warning ships about the dangerous rocks.

Philip knew he couldn't even begin to explain that the light was no longer working, so he began to run back down the spiral staircase for help.

Chapter Five

Philip took a couple of minutes getting his sleepy father to understand that there was a ship heading for the rocks. He didn't dare tell him about the ghostly figure upstairs.

Philip's father leapt out of bed and pulled open the curtains. Sure enough, the ship's lights were brighter and she was even nearer the cruel black rocks that were about to rip her open.

"That ship's in the wrong channel!" shouted Philip's father. "She'll hit the rocks."

Philip shouted back above the crashing thunder, "We'll have to phone the coastguards."

His father gazed anxiously out of the window, knowing they would arrive too late. "Yes, but we need to warn the ship now," he yelled, pulling a coat over his pyjamas. "Come on, we'll use the car headlights. Maybe the captain will see the high beam."

They quickly phoned the coastguard. Then Philip's father backed the car out of the garage and screeched it up to the headland with the headlights full on. Philip had never seen him drive so fast as the old car rocked about on the bumpy track that wound over the cliffs.

For a dreadful moment Philip thought they were going over the edge as the car skidded while his father fought to control the wheel. The car just missed going over the drop and for a few terrifying seconds Philip saw the beach below.

At the last minute, his father straightened the car and screamed to a muddy, squelching stop. Then he inched forwards, the headlights like huge eyes staring out into the storm.

But the rain was too heavy and the beam too dim to warn the ship. Philip could just make out the name on her side. *Pride of Portsmouth.*

"There's nothing else we can do," yelled his father above the storm. "Let's go back, Phil. It's no use."

Chapter Six

Reluctantly, Dad turned the car round and skidded down the track to the lighthouse. He stopped the car and ran towards the door. "I'll see what the coastguards are doing," he shouted.

When his father had gone inside, Philip turned to take one last look at the doomed ship. Then, to his amazement, he saw the waves were suddenly bathed in brilliant white light. Looking up, Philip realised it came from the lighthouse. This was impossible. It just couldn't be happening. None of the equipment worked. So how could the light shine out like this?

Philip ran back up the spiral staircase, going as fast as he dared.

When he arrived at the top, Philip felt the intense cold again and could smell brine and seaweed. Then he saw the same ghostly figure tending the light.

The ship's turning back, came the keeper's voice in Philip's mind.

I got here in time.

He was right. The *Pride of Portsmouth* was turning, slowly heading back out to sea, leaving the jagged line of foam-covered rocks behind.

"Who are you?" whispered Philip but there was no reply. *Who are you?* Philip asked again, now speaking silently, in his mind. This time the keeper seemed to hear him.

He began to move towards Philip
without making a sound, his eyes glowing
like fog-lamps, his breath so cold that it
felt like a blast of frosty air.

Philip backed away, but still the keeper
walked on, arms outstretched as if he were
searching for someone. There was
something weird about his fingers.

They were growing dark fur. Philip
could see it sprouting out of the old flesh.

Then he turned away and returned to the lamp, focusing the beam downwards towards the sea. The waiting seals were lit up by the bright light and Philip could see there was a vacant space on the highest part of the rock. Slowly the keeper began to walk towards the window.

His shape was shimmering again and Philip was suddenly more afraid than he'd ever been before. Something was happening to the keeper. The rest of his body seemed to be growing dark fur as well.

Who are *you*? Despite his fear, Philip tried to make contact again.

Chapter Seven

The figure gazed intently at Philip.

Suddenly he remembered an old photograph his father had once shown him. The ghostly figure's beard and moustache were instantly familiar.

Philip knew he was gazing into the eyes of his grandfather.

The old man turned away and strode on, walking through the glass, travelling down the lamp's beam, the wind sweeping through his fur.

The circular room was empty now. Yet the lamp was still projecting its beam. Philip ran to the window. For a moment he could see the lashing spray, the boiling surface of the angry sea that pounded the rocks. Then Philip hit the glass and fell back, winded. Struggling slowly to his feet he gazed out at the sea.

The waves parted for an instant as the big seal slid on to the rock to join its companions. Then, with a thundering roar, the surf came up again and the light went out.

Dimly, Philip could just make out the black hulk of the *Pride of Portsmouth* as she sailed safely back into the main channel.

Still shaking, Philip stared down at the foaming rock. The big seal was back and gazing up at him steadily.

Suddenly Philip didn't fear the sea any more. He knew he shared a secret with his grandfather now. In fact, for the first time, Philip felt he belonged here.

As he heard his father's footsteps on the spiral staircase, Philip picked up his grandfather's cap which was lying on the floor. The inside was wet and smelt of seaweed. Hurriedly, he put it in his pocket, just as his bewildered father reached the top chamber.

If you have enjoyed this book, why not try these other creepy titles:

The Ghost Bus by Anthony Masters

When Jack and Tina catch a late bus home from school, they realise that something is wrong. This bus is very old-fashioned, but what really gives them a fright is the passengers – they can see right through them! They're on a ghost bus, a ghost bus with a mission…

Plant Attack by Brian Morse

It looks quite harmless at first. Then the plant starts to grow, its tendrils creeping nearer and nearer, wrapping around their arms, touching their hair… Before they know it, they are trapped.

The Man with No Face by John Yeoman

Colin's bullying is getting worse. First he locks Rod in the creepy cellar; then he tells him the story of the man with no face. Rod has nightmares of scrambling in the dark; bony little hands grabbing at his ankles… The next day they return to the cellar. The thunder roars, the lights go out, and the nightmare becomes reality.

Ghost on the Landing by Eleanor Allen

It's the curse of the top landing. If any boy bullies a girl there, she can call for REVENGE. Louise almost starts to believe the ghostly tale she invents to stop Jack bullying her. There's certainly more moving up there than just ancient dust…

Storybooks are available from your local bookshop or can be ordered direct from the publishers. For more information about storybooks write to: *The Sales Department, Macdonald Young Books, 61 Western Road, Hove, East Sussex BN3 1JD.*